# Wendy the Witch

Karen

Illustrated by Brenda How

Edited by Kate Davies
Cover design by Will Dawes

# Contents

This is George and Lily and their granny, Wendy. Granny Wendy is learning to be a witch, but she hasn't been doing well in spell class. Now she's been called to see the Head Witch and Wizard.

HEAD'S OFFICE

# The Head Wizard

Granny was in trouble.
The Head Wizard glared
at her. "Your spell work is
terrible," he said. "I am
giving you one last chance
to prove you can be a
witch. You must
take a spell test
tomorrow at
12 o'clock."

**TEST SPELLS**
1 Pull a rabbit from a cauldron.
2 Get your broomstick to hover.
3 Make someone invisible.
4 Find and perform your own special spell.

BROOM STICK STAND

Percy's hat class?

"If you fail, you will have to hand over your broomstick, and leave the school."

Granny gasped and rushed from the room. In her hurry, she dropped something very important.

What did Granny drop?

# Frogs everywhere

Granny picked up her book,
and rushed home.

"We'll help you with
your spells," said Lily.

"Let's start by making
the rabbit appear."

Granny waved her
wand. Stinky slime and
leaping frogs exploded
from the cauldron. But
there was no sign
of a rabbit.

"Maybe you'd
do better with a
special spell
of your own,"
said George.

"It's worth a try," shrugged Granny. "Let's go to the Spell Library to look for a really stunning spell. But first I need to find my yellow library card..."

Can you see Granny's card?

# The spell library

When they arrived at the library, Lily felt disappointed. "Are those people really wizards and witches?" she asked.

"Yes," whispered Granny Wendy. "They're wearing disguises."

Inside the library, there were piles of dusty books, filled with spells. Most of them looked confusing and boring. But soon George spotted something he thought would help.

What has George spotted?

**WHAT'S WHAT & WHO'S WHO OF WITCHCRAFT**

**OLD SPELLS FOR SALE.** The Olde Curiosity Shoppe, Witch Way, WandsWorth.

**GREEN FROGS** and tiny toads always in stock at The Ponds, Green Witch Common.

**'SLIPPERY SLIME' TRICK.** Performed by the one & only. Miss' Ease. Tel: 9556

**WITCH HAZEL** — will magic away your warts. Cauldron Castle, Spell City.

**LOOKING FOR THAT SPECIAL SPELL?** Visit the Great Wise Wizard. Look for this sign.

9

# Star flight

"Let's go to visit the Great Wise Wizard!" said George. Granny Wendy picked up her broom.

"His castle is a long way away," she said. "We'll have to fly there. Hop on!"

They climbed onto the broomstick and held on tight. The broom jolted and jumped and zoomed into space. Soon, George started to feel sick. "I think we might be lost," he said.

"Hang on," said Lily. "Maybe one of these signposts will help!"

Which signpost should they follow?

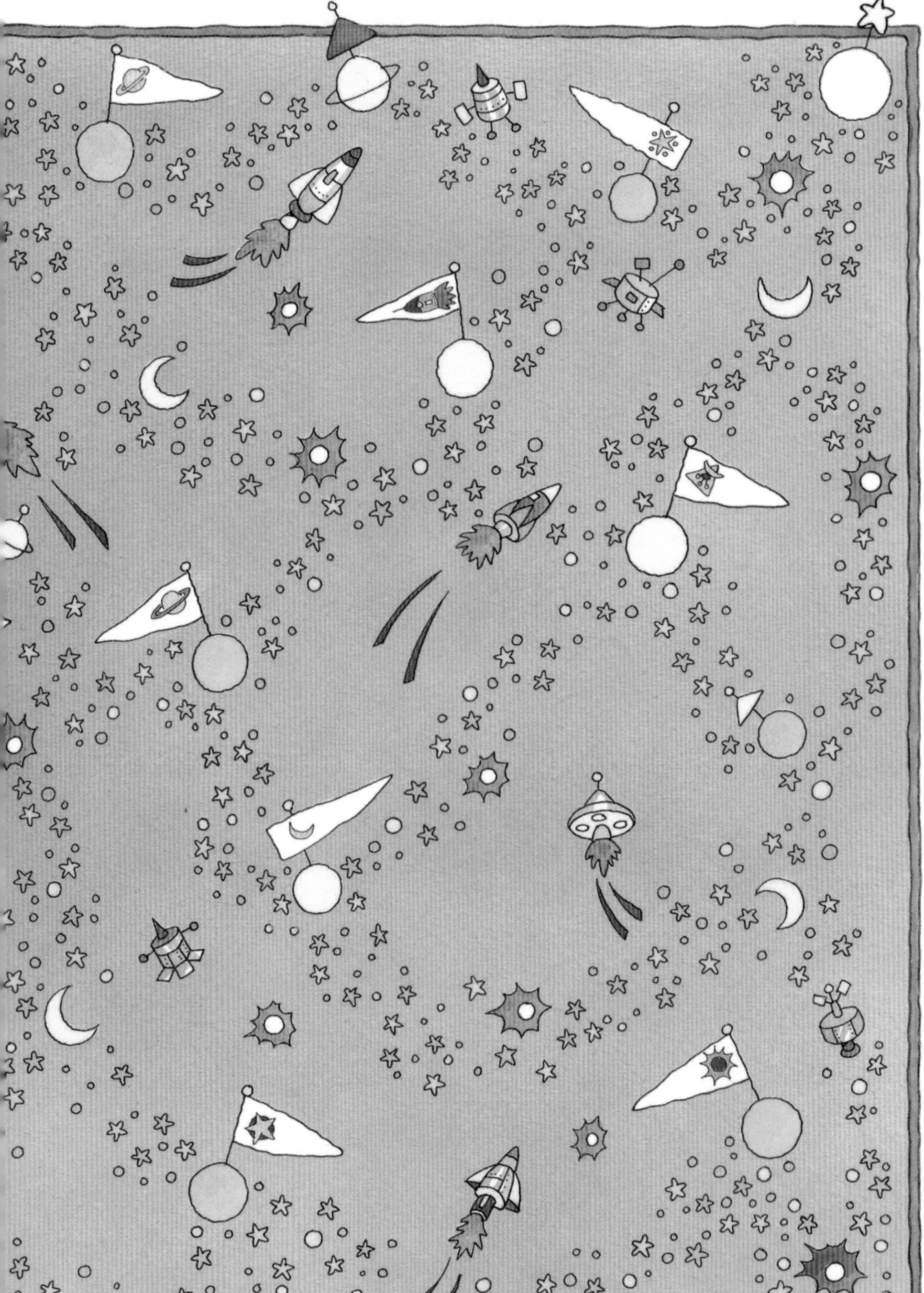

# Mysterious map

Before long, the broomstick crashed back to earth, landing next to a giant boot. Granny picked herself up and looked around.

"Oh no!" she cried. "My broom's broken!" But she fixed it with two beads from the giant shoelaces.

Then, out of nowhere, a strange bird appeared. It dropped a scroll of paper into George's hands. A glowing glass ball fell out.

Granny unrolled the paper. It was a picture map.

"That's where we are," said Lily. "And that must be where the Wise Wizard lives!"

George looked at the glowing ball. He had a feeling they were being watched...

(13)

Which is the Wizard's mountain?

# Mountain maze

George tucked the ball into his pocket, and they set off again on the jerky broomstick.

Soon they arrived at the bottom of the Wise Wizard's mountain. "The entrance is right at the top," said Granny Wendy. "My broomstick is too wobbly to fly up there, so we'd better walk. But we'll have to watch out for those red monsters!"

Can you find a way to the top?

# The ice cave

They stepped through the entrance, and found themselves in an icy cave.

Everything sparkled like diamonds.

"I can see the Wizard's castle!" shouted George, trying not to slip on the glassy floor. "But which of these paths leads there?"

Can you find the right path?

17

# The key to the castle

"Now what?" said Granny. There were four doors in the swirly purple rocks in front of them. Lily tried the handles, but all the doors were locked. Again, George had the feeling they were being watched...

Suddenly, the glowing ball
leapt from George's pocket and
sprouted three green legs.

George gasped. "I've got it!"
he cried. "I can slot the ball into
one of the pictures on the doors!
The ball is a magic key!"

Which door will it open?

# Inside the castle

When the door creaked open, they stepped, blinking, into a sunny garden. A gardener was standing in the middle of a vegetable patch, holding a sad-looking piglet.

Granny looked at the piglet, and at the half-eaten leaves on the floor. She pulled a bottle of medicine from her pocket, and poured three drops into the piglet's mouth. "He'll be back to his piggy self in no time," she said.

Lily beamed with pride. "You might have trouble with spells, Granny, but you're great with animals! Now, where's the wizard?"

Can you see the Wise Wizard?

# The book of spells

There was a puff of smoke. All
of a sudden the gardener looked
much more like a Wise Wizard.

"How nice to have visitors!"
he smiled, leading them into the
castle. "I'm Douglas. Thank you
for helping my piglet. Now, let's
see if I can help you."

Muttering a spell, he mended
the broomstick.

"The secret is getting your
magic words right," he
smiled. "That, and a little
wizard dust." He sprinkled
something sparkly over the
broomstick.

"It's your turn, Wendy" said the wizard. Granny Wendy swooshed her wand, and soon the broom was hovering in the air.

Douglas handed her a book covered in cobwebs. "I think you're ready to try a really special spell," he said, smiling. "But, first you have to work out what it says."

Can you read the spell?

gloop golden of
cup a and corn
of handfuls three
with Mix.acorn
magic a and
toadstool spotted
red a.flower

shaped bell-blue
a; teeth dragon's
two; cobweb one
Take; egg golden
a lay to goose
your get to
spell. Special

# The Enchanted Forest

"I have most of the ingredients for the spell," said Douglas, "and you can use one of my geese. But the only place to find the magic acorn, flower and toadstool is the Enchanted Forest."

They waved goodbye, and whizzed off on the broom. The Enchanted Forest was full of strange plants, but the toadstool, flower and acorn were tricky to spot.

Can you find them?

25

# Lift off!

At last, Granny Wendy had everything she needed. But it was nearly time for her test.

They leaped onto the broom, and shot above the clouds. "I feel sick!" cried Lily. They dashed past a plane, and landed with a bump as the clock struck twelve.

Granny gulped. It was time for the test. But as soon as she saw who was testing her, she smiled with relief.

Who did she see?

# Granny's test

Nervously, Granny Wendy mixed the ingredients for her special spell. Then, she pulled a fluffy rabbit from her cauldron.

She made her broom hover in the air perfectly. Next, she muttered the magic words to make George disappear.

Granny concentrated so hard that her hat flew off and zoomed around the room. Everyone stared at the hat, which was lucky, as George hadn't quite disappeared.

Lily danced in front of George's feet, as Granny fed her mixture to the goose. Time ticked slowly by. Then, at last, a golden egg appeared!

The judges held up their marks. Granny Wendy needed 25 to pass.

Has Granny passed the test?

# Granny gets it right

Granny Wendy felt fizzy with joy.

"I passed!" she cried. "Come on, let's go for a spin on my broom, to celebrate!"

They all piled on to the broom. But, before they could set off, Douglas came bounding down the steps.

"Wait for me!" he yelled. "I don't want to miss the fun!"

# Answers

## Pages 4-5

Granny has dropped her spell book. It is circled below.

## Pages 6-7

The library card is circled below.

## Pages 8-9

George has spotted something in the open book. It says that if you need a special spell you should visit the Great Wise Wizard.

## Pages 10-11

The signpost they should follow is circled below. It's the only one with Wizard's sign on it.

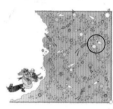

## Pages 12-13

The mountain where the Great Wize Wizard lives is circled below.

## Pages 14-15

The way to the entrance at the top of the mountain is marked here.

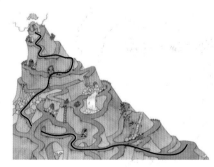

## Pages 16-17

The path to the castle is marked here.

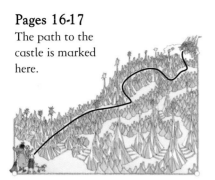

## Pages 18-19

The key will open the door circled below. The glass ball fits the picture to make the Great Wise Wizard's sign.

## Pages 20-21

The gardener is the Great Wise Wizard. We know this because he has the Wizard's symbol on his pocket. It is circled here.

## Pages 22-23

The spell is written from back to front. Start at the bottom of the right-hand page and read up. Then go onto the bottom of the left-hand page and read up. It says:

*To get your goose to lay a golden egg: Take one cobweb, two dragon's teeth, a blue bell-shaped flower, a red spotted toadstool and a magic acorn. Mix with three handfuls of corn and a cup of golden gloop.*

## Pages 24-25

The toadstool, the flower and the acorn are circled below.

## Pages 26-27

The Great Wise Wizard is one of the judges. He is the one in the middle. The Head Wizard and Head Witch are there too.

## Pages 28-29

Granny has 27 marks, so she has passed the test.